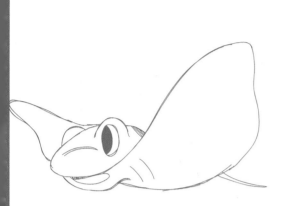

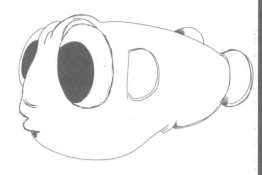

sammy stingray

sharky marky

peter puffer

walrus whippleton

bartholomew beaver

diego dolphin

For G, K, and T
Follow your dreams

This is a work of fiction. Any names are used fictitiously
or are the product of the author's imagination.
Sharky Marky was printed by:
WORZALLA
3535 Jefferson Street • Stevens Point, Wisconsin 54481
March 2015:

Summary: A shark participates in an undersea racing adventure.
IBSN: 0-9895712-0-3 (hardcover: akl.paper) [1. Shark -- Fiction.
2. Marine Life -- Fiction. 3. Racing -- Fiction.

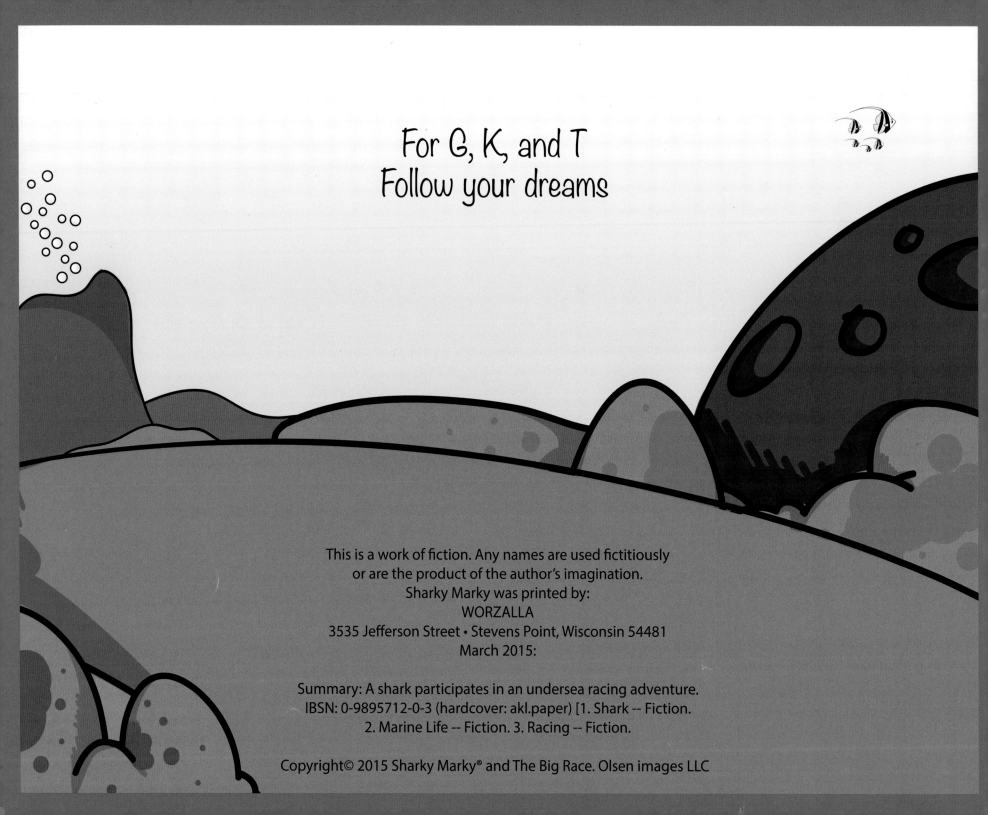

Sharky Marky

And the Big Race

Lance Olsen

Thomas Perry

At the undersea racetrack,
It's a very big day.
All the drivers are ready
To get the race underway.

Starfish Stuckey is filling
All the cars up with gas,
So the racers can *race*,
Turn, *speed*, and *pass*.

Sharky Marky is ready! It's about time to go.
Who's going to win? Sharky Marky? Maybe so.

Red Light!
Ready, steady, they're all on their marks.

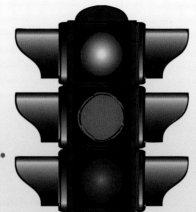

Yellow Light!
Get set, it's almost time to start.

Green Light!
It's racetime! Go, Marky, Go!

The drivers are speeding,
Marky sets the pace.
Marky's in front,
He's winning the race!

Octo Eddy's in second,
With Meanie Marlin close behind.
Those two don't race fairly,
And they will not be kind!

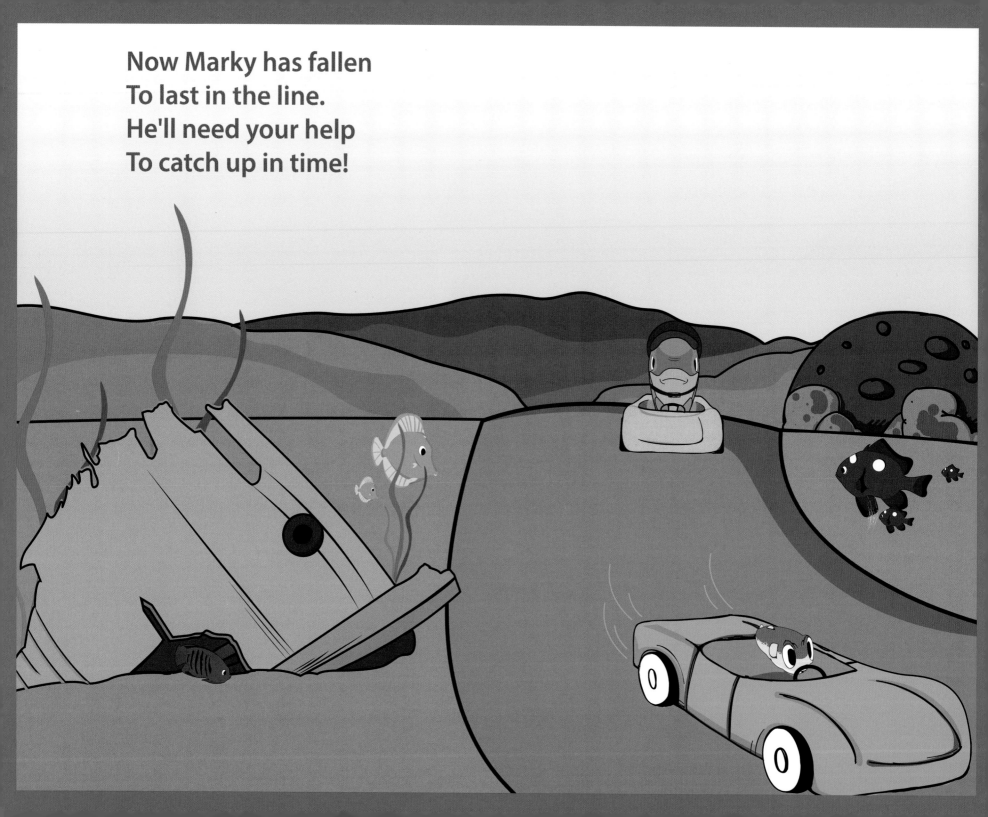

Now Marky has fallen
To last in the line.
He'll need your help
To catch up in time!

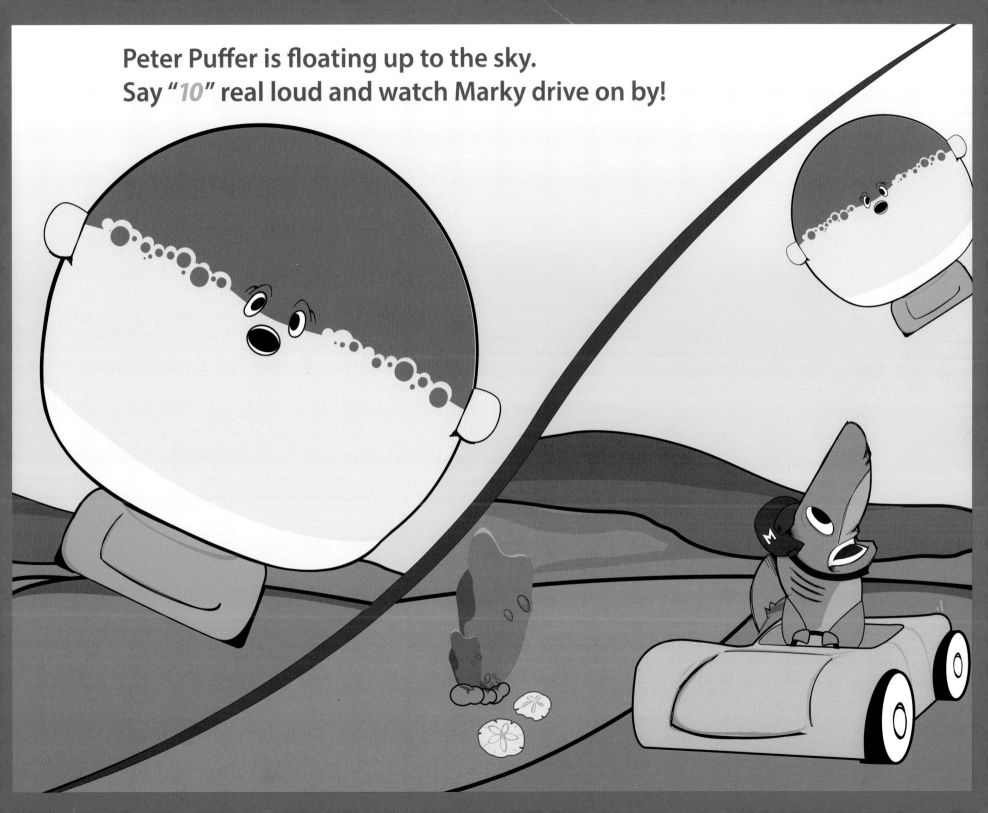

Peter Puffer is floating up to the sky.
Say "*10*" real loud and watch Marky drive on by!

Monty Moray is next and he is in the way.
Say "9" real loud and watch Marky win the day!

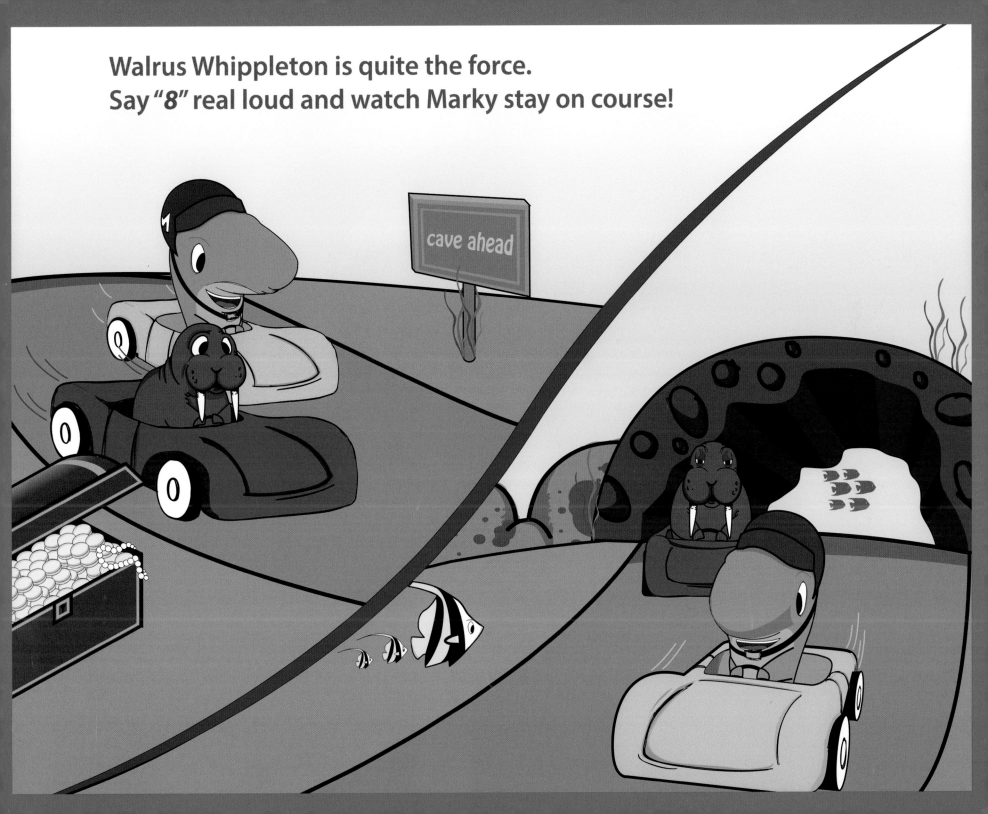

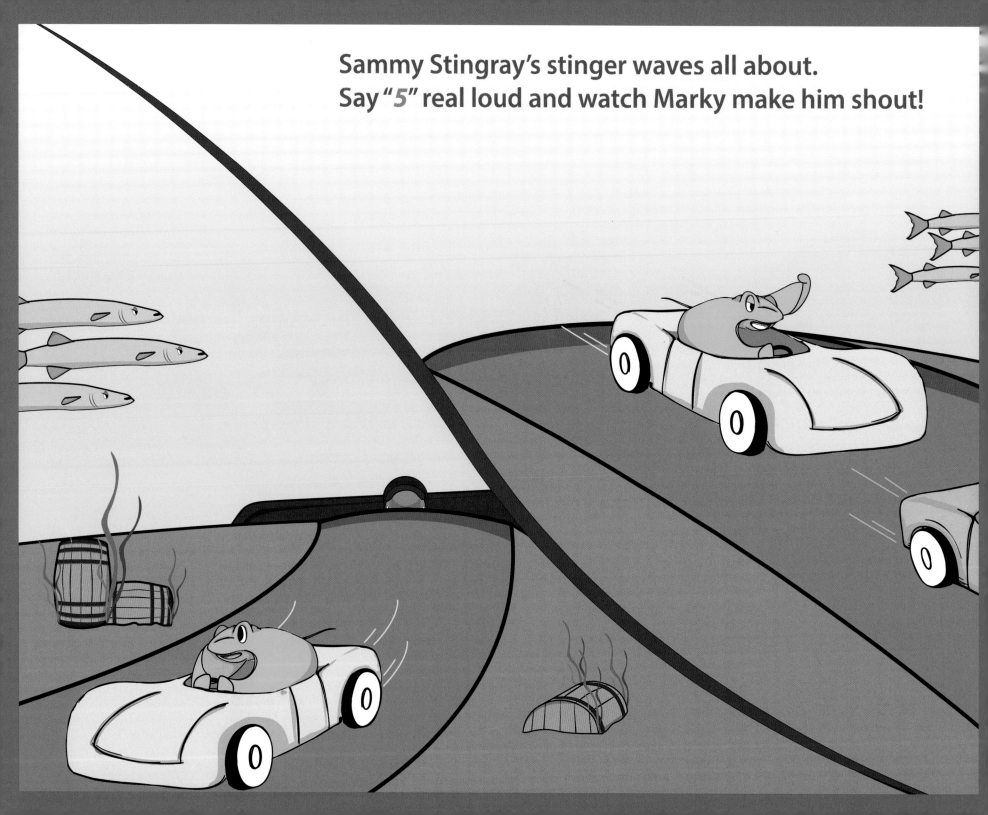

Octo Eddy is about to win the big race.
Say "*1*" real loud and watch Marky pick up the pace!

As the flag goes down,
the cars make a dash.
It's a photo finish,
the cameras all flash!

Marky's the winner! He won by a nose!
He wins the big trophy and strikes a great pose!

Sharky Marky would like to thank all his friends for making his dreams possible.

With special thanks to:

"Taz"

Ryan Normand

Allen Phillipe

Scott McCarthy

Without your help Sharky wouldn't have come to life.

killer whale karl

horace sea horse

starfish stuckey

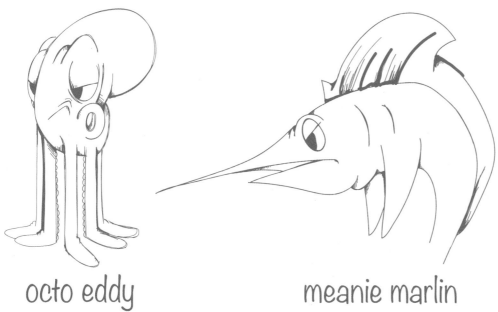

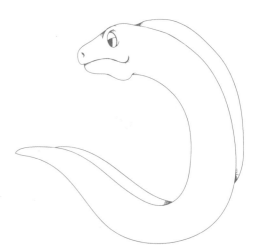

octo eddy

meanie marlin

monty moray